The Uglified Ducky

BY MAYNARD Moose

As told to
Willy Claflin

Illustrated by
James Stimson

AUGUST HOUSE
Little Folk
ATLANTA

For my wife, Jacqueline, who insisted on James—WC

For Mother Moose, from whom all stories come—MM

For J.P.S.—JS

Text copyright © 2008 by Willy Claflin
Illustrations copyright © 2008 by James Stimson

Published 2008 by August House LittleFolk
Atlanta, Georgia
www.augusthouse.com

Book design by Shock Design & Associates, Inc.
Art direction and custom text design by Graham Anthony
Audio CD recording, music, and voice-over introduction by Brian Claflin
Printed by Pacifica Communications, Inc.
Seoul, South Korea
June 2011

10 9 8 7 6 5 4 3 2 1 PB

LIBRARY OF CONGRESS CATALOGING-IN-PUBLICATION DATA

Claflin, Willy, 1944-
The uglified ducky : a Maynard Moose tale / Willy Claflin ; illustrated by James Stimson.
p. cm.
Summary: Resets Hans Christian Andersen's tale, The ugly duckling, in the Northern Piney Woods of
Alaska, where a baby moose is raised by a family of ducks who try to teach him to waddle, quack,
and fly but cannot see his true beauty.
ISBN 978-0-87483-858-9 HB
ISBN 978-0-87483-953-1 PB
[1. Fairy tales.] I. Stimson, James, ill. II. Andersen, H. C. (Hans Christian), 1805-1875. Grimme
ælling. English. III. Title.

PZ8.C498Ugl 2008
[E]--dc22
2008000974

*The paper used in this publication meets the minimum requirements of the American National
Standard for Information Sciences—Permanence of Paper for Printed Library Materials, ANSI
Z39.48-1984.*

AUGUST HOUSE, INC.
ATLANTA

GLOSSARY

Moose Words and Their English Equivalents

PARENTAL WARNING! THIS BOOK CONTAINS MOOSE GRAMMAR, SPELLING, AND USAGE, ALL OF WHICH HAVE BEEN KNOWN TO SCRUMBLE UP THE HUMAN BRAIN!

Although this text has been painstakingly translated from the original Moose, it contains many traces of Piney Woods English, a dialect generally used by Aroostic County Mooses in northern Maine.

Bandridged: bandaged

Beasties: creatures; animals, especially big lumpy furry ones

Bipedal (a Moose medical term): the state or condition of having two feet (proper for a ducky, not good for a moose)

Borned: born

Branglebush: a bush that grows in the Northern Piney Woods. Its leaves are so beautiful in the fall that beasties can often forget what they are doing and stand gazing at a branglebush for hours.

D'abandoned: abandoned, left all alone

Deflection: reflection. It should be pointed out that moose are often confused by deflections, because everything is backwards. For instance, if a moose is looking in a pond at his or her deflection and suddenly gets an itch in its right ear, it will scratch its left ear by mistake.

Demember: remember

Detention: attention

Distremely: extremely

Fambly: family

GRONK! AROOO!: These are ancient calls in the old Moose language and are difficult to translate. They mean many things:

- **GRONK**! can mean any of the following: "Look at that!" "I agree!" "My goodness!" "I see what you mean!" "Here I am!" "I'm tired!" "That looks like fun, can I try?"

- **AROOO**! can mean any of the following: "Let's go!" "Hurrah!" "Look out!" "Where is everybody?"

- When used together, **GRONK! AROOO**! usually mean something like: "OK, here I am, let's go!" But it can also mean "I'm tired! Where is everybody?"

Magnifusent: magnificent

Misdeception: misconception; a wrong idea in the brain

Quadrapedagogy (a Moose medical term): the state or condition of having four feet (just right for a moose, not good at all for a ducky)

Sogging: sopping and dripping

Tippy: to tip, especially to tip a ducky

Uglified: ugly (which you, especially, are not!)

Yug!: An ancient expression of surprise and disgust. Long ago, it seems to have meant: "I stepped on a slug!" But now it more commonly means something like, "Wow, that's distremely uglified!"

Far away in the Northern Piney Woods
there lives a storyteller named Maynard Moose.
Every full moon in the forest, the animals come from
near and far to hear him tell his Mother Moose Tales, in the
old Moose Speech used long ago. Young and old, big and
small, fur and feather, the woodland creatures gather round
    and settle down on moss
        and branch
            and log
                to listen …

Do you ever feel

like maybe you have been
borned into the wrong fambly?
Like maybe you feel like you are a little
porcupine being raised by a fambly of kangaroos—

boing! boing!

And the mommy kangaroo does not
like to have you in her pouch—**ow! ow!**
And all the other kangaroos make fun of you
because you cannot jump.

Or maybe you feel like you are a little bunny rabbit
being raised by a fambly of rhinoceroses.
Well, this is the story of a poor moose
who was raised by duckies. It is called

The Uglified Ducky.

Once upon a time

there was a little baby moose

that blunder away from his baby moosely nest,

right down to the edge of a pond.

And there at the edge of the pond was a ducky nest with five ducky eggs.
"Hmmm," say baby moose. "That looks like a snuggy place for to take a
nap. I think I will lie down there."
So the little baby moose curl up in a corner of the nest and fall asleep.

Z - Z - Z - Z - Z -

Pretty soon, the Mommy Ducky come back to check on her nest.

"Ooo, Look at that!" say Mommy Ducky. "One of the eggs is hatched already!
Yug! Look at that brown fur and hooves! That is a uglified ducky!
Boy, that's the most uglified ducky I never see!
Boy, I hope the other ones will turn out better."

And so she sit down to hatch the eggs.
And it was not long before all of a sudden

Pop! Snackle! Crack!

The eggs bust open and out pop five cute little fuzzy yellow duckies.

"Ooo! Look at that," say Mommy Ducky.
"Five cute little fuzzy yellow duckies and ...
one large and distremely uglified ducky!
Oh well. Children, it is time for you to learn
proper ducky behavior.

First, we will learn to waddle.
So stand up on your back foots and waddle after me."
So the Mommy Ducky go Waddle, Waddle, Waddle. And the five
cute little fuzzy yellow duckies go Waddle, Waddle, Waddle.
But all the Uglified Ducky can do is trip and stumble.

"No No No!"

say Mommy Ducky.

"Uglified Ducky, pay detention! This is waddle
practice! This is not practice for trip and
stumble!"

"Now children, it is time for Quack practice. Everybody line up and learn to make proper ducky sound."

So "QUACK" go the Mommy Ducky.

And "Quack, quack, quack, quack, quack!" go five cute
little fuzzy yellow duckies. But the Uglified Ducky
cannot make no Quack sound.
The only sound he can make is ...

"No No No!"

say Mommy Ducky.

"This is not practice for Gronk and Arooo!
This is Quack practice! Quack like a ducky!"
"I'm trying," say the Uglified Ducky.
But the only sound he could make was

"Gronk, Arooo!"

"You would think," say Mrs. Ducky,
"being so uglified, you would try a little harder!"

"All right, children," say Mrs. Ducky.
"Now it is time for swimming lessons.
Over to the pond we go!"

So over to the pond they go, and Sploop!
go the Mommy Ducky, and sploop, sploop,
sploop, sploop, sploop! go five
cute little fuzzy yellow duckies,

And

KASPLASH go the big Uglified Ducky.

"**MOMMY**," say cute fuzzy duckies.
"He splashed us
on purpose!"

"Now Uglified Ducky," say the Mommy, "you be
good! So everybody sit up straight and paddle!"

So off go the five cute little fuzzy yellow duckies,
paddle, paddle, paddle, paddle, paddle!
But when the Uglified Ducky try to sit up straight and paddle with his
back foots, he sink to the bottom of the pond— blub, blub, blub!

Well, when the Uglified Ducky could not hold his breath any longer, he climb out upon the bank all sogging wet and shake himself off.

"MOMMY..."

say cute fuzzy duckies.
"He splashed us again ...
on purpose!"

"THAT DOES iT!"

say the Mommy. "I don't know what's the matter with you, Uglified Ducky, but we are going to go see Dr. Quack." And so off they go to the office of Dr. Quack.

"Come in, come in!" say Dr. Quack.
"No time to lose, no time to lose!

"Oooo, Mrs. Ducky! I see you have a problem. You have
a case of uglified offspring. Please have a seat and
we will see what we can do."

"Mrs. Ducky, first thing I notice about this ducky, is that it got four foots. Four foots on a ducky you do not want. No! Do you have any other cases of Quadrapedagogy in your fambly before now?"

"No, no, no," say Mommy Ducky. "We have always been bipedal in my fambly since I can demember."

"Other problem here," say the doctor. "Do you see this? Do you see these bumps on top of the head? I am afraid your little ducky is coming down with a bad case of antlers! And antlers on a ducky you do not want, because when the antlers grow it will tippy the ducky over sideways. So we will put a tight bandridge around the head so the antlers won't grow. And because he can't make no Quack! sound, we will give him this sign to hold up that says Quack!"

So back to the pond they go with the Uglified Ducky all bandridged and holding the sign that says Quack! And the five cute little fuzzy yellow duckies begin to sing: "Ha ha-ha-ha Ha! Look at the bandridge head and the sign say Quack!"

"Oh, I hate this," say the Uglified Ducky to hisself.

Well, the days and the weeks go by,
and spring turn into summer, and the birdies go

Twerp! Cheeple!

And the thunderstorms go **Boom!**

And the days and the weeks go by, and summer turn
into fall, and the leaves on the beautiful branglebush
turn silver and scarlet and gold. And finally one
morning the time has come when duckies must
learn to fly.

"All right," say Mrs. Ducky. "Now follow me, children!"

She run along the ground and flap the wings and take off into the sky—
Zoop! And the five cute little fuzzy yellow duckies run along the
ground, flap the wings, and take off into the sky—
> **zoop, zoop, zoop, zoop, zoop!**

And the Uglified Ducky run along the ground—
> **gallump! gallump! gallump!**

But when he try to flap his front hooves, he fall down on his nose:
> **Bonk! OW!**

And all of the duckies fly off into the sky and there is
> the poor Uglified Ducky all d'abandoned
> and left alone with
> a sore nose.

"Oh, I hate this!"

say the Uglified Ducky.

"My fambly has d'abandoned me, and
my nose is sore, and I am an uglified ducky
and nobody will ever love me."

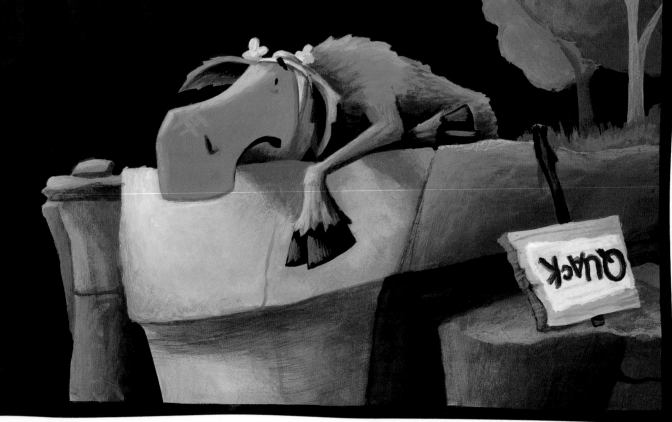

And off he go into the forest
with tears go
Sploosh!
Sploosh!

And that night he have to sleep
on sticks and rocks.

And the next day, further and
further into the forest,
feeling worser and worser ...

... until finally one morning he come to a big pond.

And there on the other side of the pond were some beautiful brown
beasties, with magnifusent antlers and fur!
"Boy, look at them beautiful beasties," say the Uglified Ducky.
"I hope they don't see me; they will make fun of me."

But one of the beautiful beasties come over and say,
"Hello! Who are you, and why is your head bandridged and you
hold a sign that says QUACK?"

"Well, that is because I am a Uglified Ducky and I cannot make
proper Quack sound, and they do not want my antlers to grow
and tippy me over."

"Oh Dear, Oh Dear —

no, no, no—you ain't no duck!" say the magnifusent beasty.
"You are a Moose! Moose is the name for the thing you would be!
Say after me—MOOSE!"

"M-m-moose?"
say the Uglified Ducky.

"Yes, indeed! Now take off this ridiculous bandridge
and check out your deflection in the pond."

So over to the pond go the Uglified Ducky and look down into the cool
clear water at his deflection: OOO! He himself is a magnifusent big
brown beastie with tiny antlers, just as beautiful as the other mooses!
"They try to trick me!" say the Uglified Ducky. "They try to trick me—
make me think I was a Uglified Ducky! I ain't no Uglified Ducky! I'm a
moose! A moose! A beautiful moose!"

And he bound off joyfully into the forest—

Boing! Boing!

And all the other mooses bound with him—

Boing! Boing! Boing!

And he is bounding joyfully through the forest ever
still, happy to be the moose that he would be!

So, if you ever feel like maybe you are a giraffe being raised by a fambly of gerbils, or a ladybug being raised by a fambly of elephants, remember—that does not mean you are uglified. No, no, no! That is a common misdeception. It just means you have not found out what you really are yet. So demember, everybody is a beautiful something or other. Especially you.

Just ask
the Uglified Ducky!